© 2016 Disney/Pixar
Published by Hachette Partworks Ltd.
ISBN: 978-1-910360-38-5
Date of Printing: December 2015
Printed in Romania by Canale

# DISNEY · PIXAR
# INSIDE OUT

## DISNEY · PIXAR
# hachette

Joy, Fear, Disgust, Anger and Sadness were the
Emotions that had guided Riley since her birth.
From Headquarters, the main control centre in
Riley's mind, they all helped the little girl make
choices in her daily life.

Every day, the Emotions made Riley's memories and stored them in the form of coloured spheres of light. With Joy in charge, she made sure there were always lots of yellow, happy-memory spheres!

In Riley's Mind World there were five Islands of Personality: Hockey, Friendship, Family, Honesty and Goofball. Riley's core memories – the most important ones – sent power from Headquarters through the lightlines to keep the islands running.

Riley's first eleven years were very happy...
but then everything changed. Riley's parents sold
their house in Minnesota, packed up and moved
the family to San Francisco!

When they finally arrived at their new home, the Emotions were horrified. The house was small and dusty and it smelled weird.

When Riley started to miss her old life, Joy was determined to keep the girl's spirits up. Joy asked Sadness to stay away from the console that drove Riley's moods.

"This is the Circle of Sadness. Your job is to make sure that all the sadness stays inside of it," Joy said.

The next morning, Joy helped everyone prepare
for Riley's first day at her new school.

Riley said goodbye to her parents and set off.

When the teacher asked Riley about Minnesota, Sadness couldn't help touching Riley's happy memory and turning it blue with regret.

Riley burst into tears in front of the whole class, and, for the first time, a blue core memory rolled into Headquarters!

Everything was going wrong! That evening, Riley had a terrible argument with her parents. At Headquarters, Joy tried to get rid of the blue core memory, but Sadness tried to stop her. As they struggled, the core memories spilled out of their holders. All of the personality islands went dark. Some of them even started to sink!

A vacuum tube sucked
Sadness, Joy and the core
memories out of Headquarters and
into the Mind World. Joy quickly
gathered up the memories.

"We can fix this," she said. "If we can
plug the core memories back in, Riley will
be back to normal."

Meanwhile, Riley was on her laptop, chatting to her best friend, Mag, in Minnesota. When Mag mentioned a new friend, Anger took over and Riley slammed her laptop shut.

Friendship Island groaned!

Joy and Sadness watched Friendship Island slip into the memory dump. It joined Family and Goofball Islands, which had already sunk into the pit.

"Goodbye, friendship," said Sadness. "Hello, loneliness."

Back at Headquarters, Anger had an idea. Since everything had gone wrong after they arrived in San Francisco, maybe Riley should run away back to Minnesota.

"Who's with me?" he asked.

Disgust and Fear agreed. Anger plugged an idea bulb into the console.

On the way back to Headquarters, Joy and Sadness discovered they shared the same favourite memory.

Joy began to understand that Riley needed Sadness in her life. If Riley didn't know Sadness, she would never know the opposite, Joy, either!

The next evening, when Riley's parents got home, they were surprised to see she wasn't back from school. They tried calling her mobile phone, but she didn't answer. She was on her way to catch a bus back to Minnesota!

At Headquarters, Anger, Fear and Disgust were regretting their plan.

"This is madness!" shouted Anger. "She shouldn't run away!" Everyone agreed.

They tried to remove the idea bulb, but it wouldn't budge.

Luckily, at that moment, Joy and Sadness arrived back at Headquarters.

"Sadness, it's up to you," said Joy, to the surprise of the others. "Riley needs you."

The Emotions watched as Sadness stepped up to the console and gently pulled the idea bulb out.

Inside the bus, Riley stood up. "I wanna get off," she said, and ran home. Riley's parents were so relieved when she walked through the front door.

Joy held out the five core memories
she had rescued. One by one, the
memories turned blue as Sadness
touched them.

Riley began to cry.

"I know you don't want
me to, but… I miss home.
I miss Minnesota,"
Riley said.

Riley's parents hugged her very tight and told her
that they both missed Minnesota, too.

At that moment, a new, blue and yellow core memory
rolled into Headquarters and settled into the core
memory holder. It was a brand-new Family Island!

From then on, Joy and Sadness worked side
by side at the console. They knew that working
together as a team was the best way to help Riley
lead a happy life.

Things were finally looking good for Riley in
her new life. At last, the Emotions could relax.
Nothing could go wrong now… at least, not until
Riley became a teenager!